Warrior Kids:

Kicking up a Storm

by

Mark Robson

First published in Great Britain in 2016
by Caboodle Books Ltd

A Catalogue record for this book is available
from the British Library.

ISBN 978 0 9933000 9 7

Cover and Illustrations by Chie Kutsuwada
Page Layout by Highlight Type Bureau Ltd
Printed by CPI Group (UK) Ltd, Croydon
CR0 4YY

The paper and board used in the paperback by Caboodle Books Ltd are natural recyclable products made from wood grown in sustainable forests. The manufacturing processes conform to the environmental regulations of the country of origin.

Caboodle Books Ltd
Riversdale, 8 Rivock Avenue, Steeton, BD20 6SA
www.authorsabroad.com

For

Mabelle Gwilliam, Kes Bryce and Sam Green.
Many thanks for all your help, and for being such fantastic role models for the Tigers.

Also, for Harry Crask, who has never let me forget that he was waiting for this book!

Also by Mark Robson

The Darkweaver Legacy Series:
Forging of the Sword
Trail of the Huntress
First Sword
The Chosen One

The Imperial Trilogy:
Imperial Spy
Imperial Assassin
Imperial Traitor

Dragon Orb
Firestorm
Shadow
Longfang
Aurora

The Devil's Triangle
The Devil's Triangle
Eye of the Storm
Convergence

Warrior Kids
Not Just for Kicks
Pull No Punches

Contents

Chapter 1 – Sparring

Charlie pressed forward his attack, but Gabriella was ready. Evading his pushing front-kick, she flashed up a front leg side-kick towards his stomach. He brushed it away with a waist block and both settled back into a fighting stance, circling one another as they each looked for an opening.

The boy looked confident. Gabriella could see in his eyes that he didn't expect much of a fight from her and she felt herself tighten inside as her determination hardened.

I'm going to wipe that smug look off your face, she thought. *Let's see how you handle this.*

The boy was rocking his weight back and forth as he circled, but where she moved lightly on the balls of her feet, he looked flat-footed and heavy. She timed her attack as his weight was shifting forwards; flicking up her front leg in a lightning fast side-kick, she aimed her foot at the slight gap between his elbow and his belt. Somehow he managed to contort so her kick failed to land, but it had always been more of a feint than a serious attempt to score. Re-chambering without

dropping her foot to the floor, she instantly pushed forwards off her standing leg and fired a second time, this time pointing her toes and aiming a turning-kick at his head. The boy was caught completely by surprise and there was a satisfying 'thwack' as her instep connected.

It would have been easy to dance away and look for the next chance, but Gabriella had him off balance and instinctively knew this was a good time to press home her advantage. Landing the foot forwards, she charged into the blitz combination she had been taught. Her back-fist strike connected with the boy's padded helmet and although he somehow blocked her straight punch to the body, she fired another quick combination of punches that scored again to the body before using her momentum to carry her out of range of his counterattack.

'Good, Gabriella!' Kai, her tae kwon-do instructor, called. 'Very good!'

Gabriella barely heard him. She was already on the attack again. The boy had been taken by surprise the first time she had pressed forward. She knew if she was to keep him off balance, she couldn't afford to let him find any sort of rhythm of his own. He was taller, heavier and stronger than she was. However, she had the edge with speed and was certain that she was more flexible than he was.

Firing a sequence of pushing mid-section side-kicks,

machine gun style, Gabriella kept him on the back foot, forcing him to retreat as she kicked again and again. Then, taking him by surprise, she gave a particularly long hop forwards and whipped an axe-kick up and over his guard to drop down at his head. Although he flinched sufficiently that his head was out of range, her foot still scored a hit to his chest and again she closed in with a rapid fire sequence of hand techniques. The boy retaliated desperately, hitting her twice on the upper arms and once to the chest before she skipped back out of reach. His punches had hurt, but she didn't make a fuss. Her guard was up and she was already looking for another opening.

'Hech-yo!'

The call to stop came as a surprise. That couldn't already be a minute, could it? She returned to her mark and faced her opponent. Kai was giving the boy a stern look. He made a hand signal, punching his right fist into his left palm.

'Warning – excessive contact. Keep it light, Charlie. We're all friends here. Another punch that hard and you'll be taking your gear off. It's not a tournament. There's no excuse for a lack of control– especially as you're sparring with one of the girls. Quick and light, understand?'

'Yes, Sir. Sorry, Sir,' Charlie mumbled.

'Are you alright, Gabriella?'

'Yes, Sir. I'm fine.'

'Good. Fighting stance – chunbi! Seejak!'

At the order they began again. The confidence had gone from Charlie's eyes now, but Gabriella stayed wary. He still had the advantage of height, reach and weight and she had used up the element of surprise. It was going to be all about keeping him at bay now. She picked up her front knee as if to kick and Charlie immediately hopped backwards. As she put the foot down without kicking he tried to counter, but was too far away. There were definite advantages to being aggressive early, she realised. Having put doubt in her opponent's mind, he was off balance and unsure of how to deal with her speed.

Charlie opted to charge at her with a blitz attempt, but he started it from so far back that she was able to evade easily, picking up another two points with a quick turning kick to the stomach as he blasted past her. Twice more he tried to press home an attack, but each time he came forward, Gabriella managed to keep him at bay either by evading, or pushing him back with her front foot.

'Hech-yo!'

This time the minute was definitely up and Gabriella was breathing hard as she returned to her mark to pay the ritual courtesies of bowing to her opponent and to the referee.

'You were great, Gee,' Abhaya whispered to her as Gabriella returned to her friend's side. 'Totally outclassed him. Go girl power!'

Gabriella instinctively giggled.

'Did you see the look of surprise when my foot smacked him round the ear?' she whispered softly. 'I don't think he even saw it coming.'

'I know. Like I said, you were a star!' Abhaya replied. 'I was rubbish. Just couldn't seem to string anything together at all.'

'You weren't rubbish, Abi. Donovan's a much tougher opponent than Charlie. He was always going to make it difficult for you.'

'At least he controls his power,' she pointed out. 'Charlie wasn't holding back, was he?'

Gabriella would have commented, but further conversation was stopped by Kai.

'OK, get your sparring gear off as fast as you can and make the rows up, people!' he shouted. 'As *fast* as you can. You have thirty seconds and then I start counting. It will be one press-up for every count after that. Go!'

Chapter 2 – I Want to Win

Kai's weekly announcements at the end of class caught everyone's attention.

'The Midlands Championships? Cool!' Gabriella breathed.

'All grades may enter. There will be competitions for both sparring and patterns at each belt level,' Kai, the senior instructor, continued. 'Black belts over sixteen years old can also compete in the destruction event.'

Gabriella Fletcher was surprised that she was allowed to compete at a regional level event despite only having started tae kwon-do a few months ago. She had a fierce competitive streak and loved nothing more than to put her skills to the test against others. This trait had served her well in many different sports at school and she often did well no matter what the competition. She glanced across at her friend, Abhaya. To her surprise she could see no reaction on Abi's face at all. Wasn't she interested in competing? Abi had gained straight A*s in her first three belt gradings. She was good – very good! Compared to others at her belt she would stand a good chance of doing well.

Donovan Richards looked more interested, but that didn't surprise Gabriella. He was more like her in many ways, though she doubted he would face the same pressures she would.

'Those wishing to enter should take a form and return it to me next week,' Kai said. 'If you need transport to Telford, let me know and I'll see to it that you get a lift there. The next grading will be the week after the competition – here, normal class time. Those who intend to grade should bring the money, together with their license, to me no later than the 15th. That's it for this week. Class, cheriots! Kyung ye!'

Everyone made attention stance and bowed at the order. A chorus of 'Thank you, Sir,' rang through the hall, accompanied by a smattering of applause and then everyone dispersed.

Gabriella immediately joined Abi, who in turn had linked up with her brother, Gurveer, and Donovan. They walked to collect their bags.

'So, what about it?' Donovan asked excitedly. 'Do the Warrior Kids head to Telford to do battle together?'

'Shh!' Abi hushed him, looking round to see if anyone had heard what he said. 'Kai told us not to call ourselves that in public.'

Donovan shrugged an apology, while Gurveer's eyes darted about nervously. Gabriella knew he was still

wary of the watcher in black whom Kai had fought on the street not far from their school. They hadn't seen him in the months since that encounter, but Gurveer was convinced they hadn't seen the last of him. Gabriella hoped he was wrong, but found the thought that they had unknown enemies both scary and yet strangely exciting at the same time.

'OK, are *we* going to head to Telford then?' Donovan corrected. 'I like the idea of seeing how we measure up to kids from other clubs. Any idea how big this event will be?'

'It's a regional event, Donovan,' Abi said with a shrug. 'There are a lot of clubs in the Midlands. There could be hundreds of competitors.'

Gabriella felt a thrill of excitement at the thought of all those people.

'Do you think you'll go, Abi?' she asked.

'Will you?'

'Definitely! Come on!' Gabriella enthused. 'You should come. Do the patterns event at least. You're awesome at patterns.'

'I'll think about it, Gee.'

Gabriella liked that Abi called her Gee. Most people shortened Gabriella to Gabby, or Gabs, but she much preferred Gee. It was cute and she felt it suited her. Besides, Abhaya liked being called Abi and Gabby was far too similar to that for comfort.

It was a strange coincidence that all four of them

were named after warriors. Until their tae kwon-do instructor, Kai Green, had pointed it out to them, Gee had not known the meaning of her name. He said that Gabriella came from the name Gabriel, an angel known as a warrior of God. Apparently, Donovan meant dark warrior, and Gurveer meant warrior of the Guru. Of the four friends, only Abhaya's first name did not directly mean warrior; it meant fearless. However, her middle name was Luann, which meant graceful warrior.

Kai didn't believe their starting at his club together was coincidence. He was convinced they were special and shared an important destiny. He had never elaborated on what he thought that might be, but he worked them hard to ensure they learned quickly and gave them constant encouragement to practise what he taught them. He was a very good teacher.

'Well, let's talk to our parents and see if they'll let us all go,' Gurveer suggested. 'I'll have a crack at it if the rest of you are going.'

Abi looked at her brother with surprise and Gee had to smother a giggle. It was rare to see Abi surprised by her brother and it tickled her that she couldn't see the competitive streak in him. He worked hard at tae kwon-do and he was good at it. Just because he did not quite have the natural athletic build and flexibility that the rest of them enjoyed did not make him any less competitive. Indeed, he had demonstrated his determination and ability at all of their belt exams so far, getting high marks each time. Gee could see him doing well in competition – especially in the sparring. With his stocky frame and determined look, he would be intimidating to many opponents.

'Hey,' he added. 'Did you hear there is going to be a new type of martial arts tournament happening in a couple of months? Apparently anyone can enter, but when you're sparring you can only hit each other with tea bags.'

'Tea bags?' Gee asked out of instinct, only realising it was one of Gurveer's jokes a split second after the words left her mouth.

'Yeah,' he drawled with a grin. 'I understand they're calling it a Tae-phoo tournament.'

The other children all groaned.

'And you have to get your parents' permission to enter because it has a PG Tips rating,' he added.

They groaned again.

'And I suppose it's being sponsored by Earl Grey and you have to camomile to enter?' Abi added.

'I like it, sis!' Gurveer chuckled. 'I'll be stealing that!'

'That's bad even by your standards, Gurveer,' Donovan said, shaking his head.

As tradition and courtesy dictated, they each turned and bowed before leaving the training hall. Gee leant in close to Abi as they unchained their bikes from the metal railings outside the Leisure Centre.

‘Do you think your mum and dad will be OK with you and Gurveer competing?’ she asked.

‘I don’t see why not,’ Abi replied. ‘Providing there are no family events planned for that weekend, of course. What about yours?’

‘Mine?’ Gee let loose one of her trademark giggles, though even Abi could hear there was little humour in it. ‘Trust me, they will be more than OK with it... providing I win, of course.’

‘Win?’ Abi laughed. ‘Just like that – win the regional championships first time out. That’s funny!’

Gee laughed with her, but the sound felt hollow in her ears. Abi clearly didn’t know her parents very well if she thought her comment had been a joke. They had been delighted to see her do so well at her gradings so far, but she knew they would push her to train harder than ever for this. Competitive did not even begin to describe them.

But that’s OK, she thought. *I won’t mind practising. This isn’t about them. I want to win this for me.*

Chapter 3 – Nothing's Ever Good Enough

Gone were the dark glasses and the long black coat. Driss had made a point of altering his appearance and clothing every week since his street encounter with Kai. Some weeks he had delegated responsibility for monitoring the children and Kai to others, but it always fell to him to keep the Master updated with their progress. He watched them pedal away from the Oxtree Leisure Centre and he sighed.

What could he report this week? Kai pushed the children in class, teaching them techniques way ahead of their belt level, but without appearing to show them too much favouritism. The instructor's subtle attention was paying off. The two boys and two girls were progressing faster than their peers. Their stances were better, their techniques stronger and their work ethic far ahead of the normal expectations of such young students. Even the chubby lad, Gurveer, moved better than many able young martial artists. Yet still Driss could see nothing that should worry a man like Master Chen.

Why the continued interest in these children? he

wondered. *Perhaps the frustrating delays in the development of the serum are forcing him to re-evaluate the danger they pose. What if it takes years for his plan to work? The children are still young, but they're growing up fast. The two boys will start secondary school in just a few short months, and the move from primary to secondary often triggers a rapid increase in maturity. They'll soon be young adults and that will change things.*

Driss leaned back in his car seat and scratched his chin thoughtfully. He didn't understand exactly what Master Chen was trying to do, but he had his suspicions. As far as he was concerned, it was not his place to question his Master's motives. He followed his boss's orders, which mainly involved ensuring company security and protecting against corporate espionage. It was only this task of monitoring Kai and the children that was out of the ordinary.

As far as the general public and the authorities were concerned, Cobra was a perfectly legitimate small pharmaceutical company. Their particular area of expertise was in developing a new range of powerful snake venom antidotes. However, Master Chen's pet personal project was one of the utmost secrecy. Every time he mentioned it, Driss's skin prickled. Whatever Chen's experiments involved, Driss suspected he was better off having no knowledge of the end goal. He'd never seen concrete evidence that the company was working on something illegal, but Master Chen did not strike him as a man bound by rules and laws. He was a man who exulted in exercising authority over others.

Whatever he's doing, his aim will be to increase his influence and power, he thought. *And I get the feeling he will do whatever it takes to get what he wants.*

* * * * *

‘Yes, of course we’ll take you to Telford, Gabriella,’ her father said enthusiastically. ‘I’m delighted to hear that your instructor encourages participation in competitions, and even more pleased that you want to go. So what will you have to compete at?’

‘I’d like to have a go at the sparring and the patterns events,’ she replied. ‘I’m not eligible to enter the destruction.’

‘Great! In that case, tell me about pattern Do San,’ Mr Fletcher said as Gabriella dumped her sparring bag under the stairs.

‘Oh, come on, Dad! Give me a few seconds at least. I’ve just walked through the door!’

‘Well, you need to know the interpretation for your grading in a few weeks,’ he pointed out. ‘And in competition, it is always best to be fully prepared. Better to have this stuff in your head now. You don’t want to be struggling to learn it at the last moment. How many moves?’

‘Twenty four,’ she replied, resigning herself to her father’s insistence. She closed her eyes and pictured the relevant page in the theory book. ‘Pattern Do San was named after the patriot An Chang Ho who lived from 1876 to 1938. He dedicated his life to the education system of Korea and furthering its independence movement,’ she recited.

‘Very good!’ he approved. ‘So can you show me the pattern before you get changed?’

'Sure,' she agreed. 'But I need a bath afterwards. Kai pushed us hard tonight and my legs feel like jelly.'

Mr Fletcher moved the coffee table from the middle of the lounge floor to make space for her and sat back on the sofa to watch. Gee took up position at one end of the space, first coming to attention, then bowing before adopting a ready stance. Looking suddenly to the left, she turned to make walking stance, throwing a powerful outward block and reverse punch combination. As she turned for the second sequence of moves she noticed that her Mum had appeared in the doorway. She was also quietly watching.

Gabriella transitioned smoothly through the trickiest part of the pattern. A straight fingertip thrust, followed immediately by a twisting release move and on into the spinning back fist strike. Concentrating on using maximum acceleration for each move, she put everything she had into every block and punch. Kai had taught her that patterns were all about making different shapes with her body, accelerating into each change and then snapping to a stop in the next new shape to make the change look sharp.

'KIYAAH!' she shouted, as she finished the pattern in a deep sitting stance with a knife hand strike to the right.

Both her mother and father clapped as she returned first to ready stance, then made attention stance and bowed before relaxing.

‘That’s looking really good, darling,’ her Mum commented, nodding and clapping enthusiastically. ‘Don’t you think, Peter?’

‘Yes, dear,’ he replied, smiling broadly. ‘That was much better than last week, Gabriella. Well done. Your walking stances still look a little narrow to me, but you have a lot more confidence and power in your moves now.’

‘Thanks, Mum. Thanks, Dad. I’m going to run a bath now,’ she said, giving her mother a peck on the cheek as she passed her in the doorway.

Trust Dad to find fault, she thought, inwardly grimacing. *Nothing’s ever good enough for him. I know he had martial arts lessons when he was younger, but it’s not like he got to black belt or anything.*

He had confused her in the first few weeks of her tae kwon-do lessons, telling her that patterns were called katas, but she now knew this to be a karate term. In Korea, where tae kwon-do originated, they were called tuls. The most annoying thing was not that he had criticised her stances, rather that he’d echoed what Kai had told her in class earlier. She decided she would try again later in front of a mirror. When she was doing the pattern it felt fine, but there must be something wrong with the way she was moving if her armchair-expert dad was picking up on it.

Chapter 4 – A Score to Settle

'Useless!' Chen muttered, shaking his head as he looked into the empty-eyed young man standing next to his leading scientist. 'A zombie! Mindless drones are of no use to me, Yunxu. I need to be able to control them without changing their character. They must be able to function normally without alerting others of a change. No one can suspect anything is out of the ordinary if we're to be successful.'

'I understand, Master,' Yunxu replied, a tremor of fear in his voice. 'We're trying, but getting the balance right is proving difficult. After the early breakthroughs, we thought refining the results would be relatively straightforward, but it's proving to be far more complex and delicate than we imagined.'

Master Chen clenched his hands into tight fists and gritted his teeth in an effort to contain his anger and frustration.

'Is the memory loss permanent?'

'There is no way to be one hundred percent certain, Master, but it does appear so. As far as we can tell his amnesia is complete and his memory is showing no

sign of resurfacing after several weeks. The latest batch of serum seems to scramble memories completely.'

'If you're certain he's not going to remember being here, have him taken to London and turn him loose,' he growled. 'I'd rather not dispose of him permanently. A trail of bodies will eventually come back to bite us and we cannot let our failures go locally, or suspicions will be aroused. The deaths of the first two test subjects were more than a little unfortunate. The police here may be lacking in resources, but they're not stupid. If we don't take the utmost care they will start to piece things together.'

'Yes, Master. I'll see to it.' Yunxu bowed and gently took the young man standing at his side by the arm and began to guide him from the Master's office.

'And Yunxu...'

'Yes, Master.'

'Let's get the next batch of subjects from further afield. We must not leave a pattern or any sort of trail that can be traced back to us. Brief Driss on what you need. He is discreet and generally efficient.'

'Understood, Master.'

* * * * *

'Hey, Gee, did you hear the one about the grasshopper who hopped into a bar?' Gurveer asked over his shoulder as they trudged up the road towards Oxtree Primary School.

'Oh, no!' Abi groaned, shaking her head. 'He's at it again.'

Gabriella giggled. 'It's OK,' she said as an aside to her friend. 'I like Gurveer's jokes. Go on, Gurveer, what about the grasshopper?'

Gurveer turned and walked backwards in front of

them, grinning. Donovan was at his side.

'The barman looked at the little creature and said "Hey! Did you know we serve a cocktail here that's named after you?"' He paused and then continued, 'The grasshopper looked surprised and replied to the barman, "You serve a drink called George?"'

Abi looked confused, but Gabriella gave her customary giggle as he turned again to walk normally next to his friend. She liked Gurveer. He was funny and even when she didn't understand some of his jokes she didn't see why Abi seemed so embarrassed by him. He was also starting to look noticeably less chubby, which had always been Abi's stated reason for the awkwardness she felt about being seen with him. Months of tae kwon-do classes combined with a growth spurt was burning away his fat.

There were some advantages to being an only child, but Gabriella had often wished that she'd got a brother or sister, if only to divert her parents' attention from being constantly on her. Not that Abi wasn't like a sister – she was great. Gabriella felt she could share anything and everything with her.

'You're crazy, Gurveer!' she called.

'I'll take that as a compliment,' she heard him say to Donovan in an aside.

Donovan laughed.

'It's as close to one as you're likely to get with jokes like that!' he replied. 'Uh oh! Don't look now, but it looks like Zach's waiting for us at the gate.'

Gabriella sighed, feeling a sinking feeling in her stomach. She didn't understand boys like Zach. What strange pleasure did he get from being nasty to people? Donovan and Gurveer had been the subject of his bullying for much of the year, but aside from a couple of minor clashes, they had successfully avoided any direct confrontations. Surely Zach wasn't stupid enough to start something now? There were parents dropping children off and teachers on duty in the playground – far too many witnesses.

Donovan and Gurveer stopped, looking unsure what to do.

'Come on, Abi,' she said softly. 'Zach's not likely to pick on us. He won't want the rest of his gang to think he's reduced to bullying girls. Let's lead the way.'

Gabriella picked up her pace and marched past the boys. Abi matched her pace. The boys followed close behind.

'Good morning, Zach,' Gabriella called cheerily as they rounded the wall and entered through the gate. 'What are you waiting here for? School's that way.'

'None of your business,' he sneered. 'Go gab somewhere else, Gabby.'

'Really? Is that the best you can do, Zach? Looks like your brain runs even slower than your legs these days. Must have been something you ate.'

Gabriella noted two of his four gang members were

struggling to keep straight faces. Where Gurveer was looking slimmer, this year had seen Zach's body balloon. He had always been big, but rather than the stocky, square-faced thuggish look that he'd had at the start of Year 6, everything about him had rounded and expanded. Only the cruel, deep-set eyes remained unchanged.

'Beat it, Fletcher... not you though, Donovan. I want a word with you.'

Marcus appeared, running across the playground towards them.

'Hi, guys!' he called. 'Are you coming, or what?'

'Get lost, traitor!' Zach growled. 'Donovan's coming with us, ain't you, Donovan? Unless of course he's going to hide behind a little girl.'

Zach's gang had the gateway well covered. Donovan would struggle to slip through their net unless someone created a hole for him, Gabriella noted. She looked round for the teacher on playground duty, but found she couldn't see him anywhere.

Gabriella suddenly felt a pulse of heat from the special ring Kai had given her. It raced up her arm and spread through her body.

'Don't be stupid, Zach,' she heard Donovan warn. 'I don't want to fight you, but you know I will if I have to. Don't you remember what happened last time I hit you?'

'You won't touch me,' Zach sneered. ''Coz if you do, you'll be banned from learning your precious martial art. See, I found out that you're on your final warning. You won't do nothin', posh boy.'

The bully did a quick scan to make sure the playground was still clear of teachers. It was.

'Grab him, lads!' he ordered. 'And take him behind the changing rooms. I've got an old score to settle.'

That was when it happened...

Chapter 5 – The Kick

Gabriella allowed her eyes to focus on the middle of Zach's body, just as Kai had taught her, but then it was as if everything happened in slow motion. The bully stepped forward, his right arm extending to brush her aside so that he could get at Donovan, but she was already in motion. Dropping her school bag, she side-stepped to the right to give her a clear path to her target, drew her left leg up into a chamber position and angled her foot to drive the outside edge of it upwards into Zach's gut.

'Geeeee! Noooo!'

Abi's voice also seemed slow and echoing as her foot found its target. Gabriella had fired the front leg kick with a reasonable amount of power, but at the moment of impact something very strange happened. The surge of heat from her ring that she'd felt rush through her body suddenly flooded out along her left leg to her foot and there was a silent explosion of force like an intense electrostatic shock that caused her leg to recoil.

Still in slow motion, Zach's mouth contracted into a

small 'O' shape and he exhaled with an exaggerated 'OOOOOFFF' sound. Gabriella watched with stunned amazement as Zach's bulk was plucked off the ground and hurled through the air to crash into two of his gang members. The three boys went down in a tangled heap. It should have been her who had been driven backwards, kicking into someone so much heavier, but she remained balanced on her right leg, fists up in a guard and her left leg re-chambered, ready to fire out another kick.

As Zach and his two friends hit the ground, the world returned to normal speed.

'Time to go,' she said quietly, heart racing and body still tingling as she looked round at the others and beyond to see if anyone else had seen what just happened. It appeared she'd been lucky.

'Wha... what? Gee...?' Donovan gasped.

Zach was on the floor groaning and clutching his stomach. The two members of Zach's gang who were still on their feet were already circling warily behind their fallen friends, keeping their distance from Gabriella.

'Later, Donovan,' she said. 'These boys will keep their mouths shut. I don't think they'll want us to spread the word that they're scared of a year five girl, will you boys?'

Zach's gang members shook their heads, flinching as she narrowed her eyes and took a step towards

them. Zach was too immersed in rolling around on the floor to hear her.

'I should warn you that Donovan and Gurveer kick much harder than I do,' she added. 'I did Zach a favour today. If I'd let one of them hit him, he wouldn't be getting up any time soon. I suggest you leave me and my friends alone in future.'

Gabriella picked up her school bag and marched past the gang. Abi, Donovan and Gurveer followed in shocked silence behind her. The ring on her finger, which a moment ago had pulsed with energy, was cooling back to a more normal temperature.

'Two things, Gee,' Donovan said urgently once they were out of earshot. 'One: Kai is going to be *SO* mad with us. And two: *how the heck did you do that*?'

'I've no idea,' she replied excitedly, smiling as she was sure she detected a hint of jealousy in his voice. 'But it felt amazing! I think it was the ring that Kai gave me. Did anyone else feel theirs get hot?'

'Yes.'

'Yes!'

'Me, too!'

'It was weird,' Gabriella continued. 'As I kicked, it was like the heat from the ring shot along my leg and out through my foot. I should have bounced off him, but did you see Zach fly?'

'I'm not going to forget it ... ever!' Abi said, her voice full of awe. 'It was like something out of the movies!'

'I don't think Zach's going to bother you any more, boys,' Gabriella noted, and then giggled as the image of the bully's shocked face as he left the ground filled her mind's eye once more.

'You think!' Gurveer said sarcastically.

'I've dreamt of doing something similar to him for a long time,' Donovan admitted. 'But Zach was right. I didn't want to risk losing my lessons in tae kwon-do.'

'Talking of dreaming, do you know what I don't get?' Gurveer asked. 'Teachers are always telling you to follow your dreams. "Dream big," they say... but then they get upset if you fall asleep in class! What's with that?'

Donovan, Abi and Gabriella all groaned.

'We're going to have to tell Kai about this, Gee,' Abi said. 'He might be able to explain what happened, but he's not going to be happy.'

'It should be OK,' Gabriella said thoughtfully. 'After all, I was just following the tae kwon-do oath.'

'Oath?'

'It's in the front of your tae kwon-do license,' she said. 'We're supposed to promise to follow the rules and show respect to our seniors, but the last part of it says that we should never use tae kwon-do except in self-defence, or in defence of the weak, so I'm good on both counts.'

'You cheeky...!' Donovan began, his eyes widening.

Gee giggled again, and Abi laughed with her.

'Boys!' Abi chuckled. 'No sense of humour.'

'This from the sister who has no respect for my jokes,' Gurveer muttered, shaking his head. 'It's wrong... just wrong!'

Gabriella regarded Abi and Gurveer for a moment as she wondered again how different life might have been if she'd had a brother or sister. Her body was still tingling with the after-effects of the power surge she'd felt from the ring, but for a moment she also felt as though she had something missing inside. Was this normal? Did Donovan feel the same way? If he did, he didn't show it. She envied the gentle rivalry between Abi and Gurveer.

Suddenly a thought occurred to her. Why hadn't the ring given her extra power and speed during their sparring in class? She'd been wearing it under her gloves when she'd been sparring with Charlie, yet she'd felt nothing out of the ordinary and he had actually been hitting her. So what had triggered the rings today? It was yet another layer to the mystery.

Chapter 6 – Something Unusual

'What is it, Driss?'

The Master was sitting behind his desk, staring intently at one of the many cobras coiled in tanks around his office. He had been particularly bad-tempered in recent weeks. How would he take more bad news? Driss was not looking forward to finding out, but he knew that holding back this information would likely anger him even more.

'It's about one of Kai's students, Master,' he began. 'One of the girls.'

'Yes?' Chen replied, his attention shifting from the snake to regard Driss with a cold, penetrating stare. 'What about her?'

'You said to tell you if I noticed anything unusual about them,' Driss continued. 'Well, it seems young Gabriella Fletcher has more to her than meets the eye. If I hadn't seen it with my own eyes, I wouldn't have believed it possible.'

'Tell me,' Chen urged, his eyes narrowing. 'What did this girl do to leave you so amazed?'

'Master, she faced off against the school bully, a lad

who must weigh at least twice as much as she does, and floored him with a single side-kick...'

'She has been well trained by Kai,' Chen interjected. 'A well-placed kick against anyone with no training could incapacitate them.'

'I agree, Master, but it was the power of her kick. It was... well... it was impossible!' Driss shrugged, unable to think of another way to describe it. 'Her kick literally picked the boy off his feet and hurled him two metres through the air. It was bizarre! By all rights she should have bounced off him. It was almost as if the laws of physics didn't apply to her.'

The Master's shoulders tensed. Driss could almost see his thoughts whirling behind his dark eyes as he digested this information. His lips tightened into a thin line.

'Interesting,' he said slowly. 'And you're sure it wasn't just a trick of perspective...'

'Positive, Master.'

Chen curled his right index finger thoughtfully across his lips and his eyebrows drew together in a frown. Driss felt a shiver run down his spine. If he didn't know better, he could have sworn that the Master was radiating a cold aura into the heat of his office.

'I think it's time we dealt with these young warriors,' he said slowly, his voice like ice. 'The prophecy spoke of four. If they cease to be four, then the prophecy cannot be fulfilled. Bring one of them to me. I'm in need of more test subjects for the next batch of my serum. Let's start with this girl, Gabriella.'

'That will not be easy, Master,' Driss replied, a wave of fear descending through his body. 'Kai's people are watching them constantly. I doubt I could do it alone. I would need a diversion of some sort.'

'Take others if you must, but make it happen,' Chen ordered. 'I'm counting on you, Driss.'

'Yes, Master,' Driss replied, bowing. He paused a moment. 'Do you need the girl immediately?' he asked.

'What are you thinking?'

'The children are planning to compete in the Midlands Tae Kwon-do Championships,' he said thoughtfully. 'There will be well over a thousand people there. It should be easier to separate her from the others in such a crowded place.'

'Very well,' the Master agreed. 'Do it.'

* * * * *

'I thought you were more sensible, Gabriella,' Kai said sternly, his face cold and emotionless. 'I didn't think I'd need to give you the warning I gave to Donovan last year.'

'Sir?' she asked, stopping abruptly a few paces short of the door to the training hall.

How did he find out? she thought, horrified. *Zach didn't say anything to the teachers. Had he come running to Kai instead?*

'You all promised me that you wouldn't use your skills outside class,' he continued, his eyes scanning across those of Donovan, Gurveer and Abhaya before returning to meet hers. 'What do I need to do in order to get it into your heads that you *must not* use tae kwon-do outside of the training hall?'

'But, Sir,' Gabriella protested. 'It was self-defence. Zach started it. He moved to hit me. I side-stepped and instinctively hit him with a front leg side-kick. I didn't mean to hurt him – I just wanted to make him wary enough to let us past without any trouble.'

'I've heard about the kick,' he said, his eyes narrowing slightly as he again scanned across the faces of the four children. 'We will talk privately about that after class. You could have seriously injured that boy, Gabriella. And then what would you have done? You were lucky this time. Don't let there be a next time! Now get yourselves into the dojang and start warming up.'

'Yes, Sir.'

When the lesson began, Gabriella found her mind wandering. How did Kai know about the incident at school? She tried to imagine Zach coming here to tell on her, but that didn't fit with what she knew about the bully.

'Look lively, Miss Fletcher!' The prompt from Wayne was enough to grab her attention. 'On the spot, inwards block, back fist strike, front leg side-kick… hanna… dool…'

Mr Abbot rattled out the orders at machine gun pace, and Gabriella's competitive streak overcame her curiosity. Her focus shifted to concentrating on the instructions, and performing the techniques with as much speed and power as she could. There was no way she was going to let the boys outshine her. The only way to improve was to give one hundred percent effort, one hundred percent of the time and she wanted to prepare as best she could for the Midlands Championships.

To her disappointment there was no call for the students to put on their sparring gear and the lesson focused entirely on patterns, line work and non-contact set sparring drills. She had hoped to spar again tonight. Kai called all the groups back together for a warm-down for the final five minutes and then lined them all up by rank as he ran through the weekly notices before ending the class. There was another reminder to hand in entries for the Midlands Championships.

'… Gabriella, Abhaya, Donovan and Gurveer, please remain after class. I'd like a word with you before you go, please. Class, cheriots! Kyung ye! Dismissed.'

Many of the students called out 'Thank you, Sir!'

and there was a polite smattering of claps from the scattering students as they moved to pick up their gear and leave.

Kai waited until everyone was out of earshot before he began. His face was stern and Gabriella's heart sank as they waited in silence. It suddenly occurred to her that he might stop her from competing as a punishment for fighting outside of class. The thought that her three friends might get to go to the Midlands Championships without her set her hands trembling. He wouldn't be that mean, would he?

Chapter 7 – The Midlands Championships

Kai's face gave nothing away. Gabriella could not tell if he was angry, thoughtful or disappointed. If anything, he looked as if he was daydreaming.

When she had recounted her version of the events with Zach, she couldn't help thinking it sounded like something from a TV programme. Especially the strange energy rush and Zach flying through the air.

'I'm sorry, Sir,' Gabriella sighed. 'I know we shouldn't use tae kwon-do outside of class. To be honest, I didn't expect Zach to grab at me like he did. I reacted on instinct.'

'Apology accepted,' Kai replied. 'I'm sure you did not intend to hit him as hard as you did. However, the incident has raised some issues that I, and all of you, need to think about. First, you can now see why self-control is so important and why we stress it so much in class. If you had seriously injured Zach, you would have been in trouble with the Police and could have been charged with a serious crime. You would certainly have lost your tae kwon-do license and would no longer be allowed to train with us.'

'I know, Sir. And I really don't want to stop coming to training. I love tae kwon-do. It's great fun.'

'To be fair to you, it seems that the power of your kick was boosted somehow by something unnatural,' Kai continued. 'I suspected the rings Master Lin gave me were for more than decoration, but I did not foresee this. My concern now is the safety of my other students here at the club. Perhaps it's better that you don't wear them in class.'

'Sir, the ring didn't react when I was sparring with Charlie the other week. I don't think it will react just because someone is hitting me. It got hot when Zach came at me. If you remember, the boys said their rings got hot when the man in black chased them. I think the rings must sense danger somehow.'

Kai considered this for a moment, then shook his head. 'I can't risk it,' he said. 'I know I told you to wear the rings at all times, but I must put safety first – not just yours, but that of all my students. You might be right about how the rings work, but we don't have enough evidence to prove it. Please take them off before we start class and put them on again afterwards.'

'And at the Midlands Championships?' Donovan asked.

'Yes,' Kai confirmed. 'You wouldn't want to hit someone that hard by accident there. Aside from the potential danger to your opponent, it would also result in your immediate disqualification and I'm sure you don't want that.'

'No, Sir,' they all chorused.

'Then it's decided,' Kai said. 'Exploring the power that the rings give you is not an option if we have to put you in danger to activate them. Keep training hard. You're all doing well and I'm proud of you. Keep the rings a secret. We do not want Chen finding out about them.'

'Yes, Sir.'

* * * * *

'Wow! Look at all those people!' Gabriella breathed as they drove past the entrance to the sports centre.

A huge line of people, many wearing their white tae kwon-do suits, were queuing outside the main doors, down along the ramp and right round the corner of the building. Some were chatting and laughing, while others were making a show of staying warm.

'Perhaps we should have got here a bit earlier, Dad,' she added in a louder voice as they turned into the car park.

'Nonsense,' he replied. 'We're in plenty of time. They haven't opened the doors to admit the competitors yet. You don't want to be standing about for too long out there. You'll only get nervous standing in the line.'

'Look!' Gabriella said excitedly, pointing between the two front seats. 'There's Abi and Gurveer! They must have just arrived.' Winding down the window, Gabriella leaned out and waved to catch their attention and Abi's face lit up at the sight of her friend.

Moments later they were parked. Gabriella was out of the car in a flash, holdall in hand and fretting impatiently to catch up with the others. They joined the queue some way back from Gurveer and Abi, but the Chaudhry family were quick to give up their places in the line and move back so that the children could wait together.

Gabriella's stomach was churning like a washing machine.

'Everyone looks so confident,' she whispered to Abi.

'I know!' she replied. 'It's not fair! I feel so tense that I might explode at any moment.'

'You didn't have cheese on toast for breakfast, did you, Sis?' Gurveer asked.

'No, why?'

'Well I was just thinking about that cheese factory that exploded in France recently,' he said. 'Very messy! De Brie went everywhere.'

'I didn't hear about...' Gabriella began. Then she stopped and groaned as she got the joke. 'That is truly terrible, Gurveer! Where do you get them from?'

'Oh, here and there,' he chuckled.

'Aren't you nervous?'

'Yep, but I find that telling jokes helps to calm me down,' he replied. 'You?'

'More excited than nervous at the moment,' she replied. 'But that will probably change once we get inside. Have you seen any sign of Donovan, or Kai?'

'Not yet.'

'I expect Kai's already inside,' Abi suggested. 'I've seen several other referees walk straight to the top of the line. And if Donovan isn't ahead of us, I'm sure he'll be here soon.'

'Talking of lines,' Gurveer said. 'What do you call a line of girls' dolls, Gee?'

'No idea,' she replied.

'A Barbie-queue.'

Both girls groaned.

'Don't you know any jokes that are actually funny, Gurveer?' Gabriella asked.

'My jokes *are* funny!' he insisted. 'You just don't have a sense of humour. Anyway, you shouldn't criticise someone unless you've walked a mile in their shoes... that way when you do criticize them, you'll be a mile away *and* you'll have their shoes!'

Gabriella giggled.

'OK, that was sort of funny,' she admitted.

Suddenly they became aware that the line ahead was moving. The Midlands Championships were ready to begin. Excitedly, the three friends shuffled forward, parents close behind them.

Across the street a watchful pair of eyes followed their progress towards the door from the sanctuary of his car. Like a gigantic caterpillar entering the sports centre, waves ran along the line as sections of the queue expanded and contracted. Driss took a deep breath. He had acquired his target and identified the adults he needed to avoid. Gabriella and her two friends disappeared in through the main doors. It would be easy enough to find her competition square once he was inside. Separating her from the others might be tricky, but he felt sure that if he was patient, he would get his chance to take her.

Chapter 8 – A Prickle of Danger

'G. Fletcher... G. Fletcher...'

'Yes, Sir!' Gabriella called out, jumping up to her feet and stepping out into the square. On the other side, a second referee was calling another name. There were about fifty girls sitting around the edges of Area 14, ranging in age from about six to fifteen years old. That was the strange thing with performance patterns competitions – there was a vast maturity range among the competitors. As this was a big division, the square had been divided into two for the first round.

Gabriella concentrated on the three seated figures dressed in black sitting in front of her. She took her position on the 'T' shaped marker.

'What pattern are you going to do?' the referee asked.

'Pattern Do San, Sir,' she replied.

'PATTERN DO SAN,' he called to the judges. 'Cheriots! Kyung Ye! Chunbi! Pattern Do San, twenty four movements, in your own time... SEE JAK!'

The next thirty seconds went by in a blur. She tried

to remember all the advice that Kai had given about performing patterns in competition, but the excitement of the moment took over. As she finished with a powerful knife-hand strike in sitting stance, she realised that she had rushed it. Her heart was pounding and her mouth was dry.

'Cheriots! Kyung Ye!'

Gabriella snapped to attention and bowed before turning to return to her place at the edge of the square.

'Judges, show,' the referee called.

The three judges lifted their score cards. They all said the same: nine point five. Respectable, but not high enough to win. She sat back down next to Abi, disappointed and more than a little frustrated.

'Good pattern, Gee,' Abi said, patting her arm.

'Nah, I rushed it,' she whispered back giving an automatic giggle. 'I got carried away. Wish I could do it again.'

It was just as Kai had told them – scoring well in performance patterns was more about showmanship than knowledge of the pattern, or sheer power. They sat quietly for several minutes watching as others were called forward for their chance to impress the judges.

'A. Chaudhry... A. Chaudhry.'

'Yes, Sir,' Abi called out.

'Good luck, Abi!' Gabriella called after her. 'And don't rush!'

Abhaya also chose to perform pattern Do San. Although she could not compare her friend's performance with her own, Gabriella could appreciate the quality of Abi's rhythm, power and technique. This was her strongest discipline, and she looked very good.

'Judges, show,' the referee called.

Two nine point sixes and a nine point seven, Gabriella noted. It was one of the highest scores so far.

'Well done, Abi! You were brilliant!' she said, still clapping as her friend returned to sit next to her.

'I wouldn't have done so well if I'd gone before you,'

she replied modestly. 'I would have raced if you hadn't reminded me at the last second.'

'Nonsense!' Gabriella said firmly. 'You've always had a better feel for patterns than me.'

Watching the judges score the rest of the competitors was quite exciting with Abi having posted such a strong score. When all of the children had performed, the referees got together at the judges' table to select the top few scores from each side of the square to perform again in front of a larger panel of five judges. Eight girls were called – four from each side. Sure enough, Abi was among them, but despite knowing that her score hadn't really been good enough Gabriella still felt a pang of disappointment when her name wasn't called. She glanced up at the crowd to where her mum and dad were sitting and shrugged. Her dad didn't look happy, which made her feel even worse. What would he say when she got back up to them?

The final round was very competitive. All of the girls looked strong, but there was little doubt that Abhaya was one of the best and when it came to handing out the medals, Gabriella was delighted to see her friend win silver.

'Wow! That's a really nice medal,' she enthused as she gave her friend a hug. 'Well done, Abi!'

'Your turn next, Gee,' she replied with a grin. 'You're going to do well in the sparring, I'm sure.

Come on. Our next competition isn't going to start for a while, let's go and see how the boys are doing. They're over on square three, I think.'

'Sounds good,' Gabriella agreed. She gave her mum and dad a quick wave before slinging her sparring holdall over her shoulder and following Abi into the crowd. It wasn't easy to move, but staying close together they threaded through the press of people around the edge of the gigantic sports hall.

As they squeezed through the crowds, Gabriella began to feel uneasy. At first she thought it was just the lack of space and the noisy surroundings. However, as they got closer to the square where the boys were competing, the prickling on the back of her neck became more intense and she began to look round nervously. They arrived at square three just in time to see the medal ceremony and Donovan collecting a bronze medal.

'Yay! Way to go, Donovan!' Abi yelled, clapping enthusiastically.

Gabriella also clapped, but her focus was not on the square. There was danger here. She felt breathless. Trapped. She reached into the end pocket of her bag and rummaged through the contents until she found the little velvet bag which held the special ring that Kai had given her. Taking it out she put it on and immediately felt a lot better. The ring felt warm to the touch, but not hot like it had been when Zach had attacked her. If there was danger, it wasn't immediate. Was the metal warm through having been kept in the velvet bag?

'Abi?' she asked, tapping her friend on the shoulder.

'Yes.'

'Have you got your ring with you?'

'In my bag,' she answered. 'Why?'

'Something's not right,' she replied. 'I don't know why, but would you mind putting it on for a bit? I think we should be wearing them.'

'Sure, if it makes you feel better, Gee.'

'Thanks, Abi,' she said, taking another quick look round the hall. 'Any idea where Kai is? It would be good to tell him how well you and Donovan have done.'

'Good idea. He's refereeing on square six, I think,' Abi replied with a happy grin. 'Let's get the boys and go now.'

Gabriella knew she'd be more comfortable with Kai nearby. Maybe she was just feeling bad because she wasn't looking forward to facing her dad's disappointment, but she didn't think so. The prickle of danger wasn't going away. If anything it was getting stronger.

Chapter 9 – Attacked!

Driss shadowed the girls through the crowd, keeping his distance without losing them. His target, Gabriella, appeared wary. It was almost as if she knew he was here. She looked round more than once, her eyes scanning the crowds, but her gaze slid past him without pause. He was fairly certain she'd not noticed him.

Just relax, Gabriella, he thought. *Enjoy the competition. Don't make this any more difficult than it needs to be.*

He was hoping to snatch her between competitions, but so far there had been no opportunity. He knew his best chance would be to catch her when she visited the café or the toilets, but so far she had shown no sign of heading out from the main competition area.

Patience, Driss, he told himself, fingering the small bottle of chloroform wrapped in cloth inside his pocket. *Keep your distance and wait. Your chance will come.*

* * * * *

Kai's face lit up with a broad smile and he gave them a 'thumbs up' signal when he spotted Abi and Donovan holding up their medals at the barrier next to the competition square. The competition on his square had just completed and the umpires were gathering the competitors for the next one. Over the tannoy the children heard the announcement.

'Boys... blue belt... patterns... Area 6. Boys... blue belt... patterns... Area 6...'

'Well done, Abi! Well done, Donovan!' he said, clearly delighted at their success. 'Medals at your first competition! I'll be honest, I thought you'd do well, but most students are too nervous to medal on their first competition. Fantastic!'

'Have you any idea how long we have until the sparring starts, Kai?' Gabriella asked.

'I'm not sure exactly, but I imagine you should have at least half an hour,' he replied. 'The girls' green belt patterns competition on your square will take a while longer yet, girls. The boys will be similar. Try to find a bit of space somewhere that you can stay warm. Maybe do a little shadow sparring, but be careful not to overdo it. You don't want to be tired when you face your first real opponent.'

'Will do, Sir,' Donovan answered. 'And thanks for telling us about this competition. It's really fun!'

Kai returned to organising his square.

'Can I have a proper look at your medal, sis?' Gurveer asked.

Abi held it up for him to see and he weighed it in his hand for a moment. It was large and heavy on a red, white and blue sash.

'Nice,' he said, giving her a nod and a smile. 'It looks just like the one my mate won for swimming... and you wouldn't believe the lengths he went to for his!'

Abi gave him a friendly punch, while Gabriella and Donovan just groaned.

'Come on, guys,' Donovan urged. 'Let's do as Kai suggested and find somewhere that we can keep moving.'

The four weaved back through the crowds. Abi and Donovan diverted off up into the spectator stand briefly to show off the medals they had won to their parents. Gabriella and Gurveer continued round the end of the stand, out into the corridor and along to the reception area where there was some open space.

'Just going to visit the boys' room while I have a chance,' Gurveer told her. 'But in keeping with where I'm going, I'll leave you with these words of wisdom from my Gran: Life is like a roll of toilet paper – the closer you get to the end, the faster it goes!'

Gabriella giggled. Gurveer was a quirky character. She couldn't help thinking that she would have liked him even if he hadn't been her best friend's brother. She watched as he disappeared through the door into the toilets and then turned to walk towards the large glass windows at the front of the Sports Centre reception area.

Everything happened at once. Her ring suddenly burned hot on her finger and she gasped. An instant later a man's hand clamped a damp cloth across her face, pulling her backwards. Her lungs were full of air from having sucked in a large breath and her first instinct was to scream, but the cloth muffled her effort. Then her conscious thoughts caught up and Kai's special lesson on escaping an attacker flashed into her mind.

All at once she allowed her body to go completely limp, catching her assailant by surprise. He was braced for a struggle, not dead weight. Although she was not very heavy, her attacker was unprepared for her

unexpected collapse and she slipped down through his grasp and on to the floor. The moment she hit the ground, she rolled to the side and spun her body round to kick hard at the back of his ankles.

Even as she kicked, Gabriella looked up into the eyes of her attacker. It was the same man who had threatened Gurveer. The man who Kai had warned to stay away. A surge of power from her ring raced through her body just as it had when she had kicked Zach. Time seemed to slow and her foot connected. Once again the impossible suddenly became a reality.

She felt the silent explosion as her foot hit him and her leg recoiled as the man's feet flew out from under him.

Snapping back into real time, Gabriella used the recoil force from the impact to help her roll away as the man landed hard on his back. His head smacked on to the floor with a loud crack. Gabriella didn't stop to see if he would recover. She sprang to her feet, turned and ran back towards the main hall.

'Hey, you! Stop!' she heard. It was a man's voice who shouted, but she didn't know if it was her attacker or someone else. Either way she had no intention of obeying the order.

She ran, sprinting back along the corridor. As she approached the main entrance doors to the Competition Hall, the official at the entry desk put out a hand to slow her down.

'Wrist band?' he asked.

Gabriella slowed to a stop, panting. She felt dizzy. A strange smell haunted her nostrils. Whatever had been on the cloth must have rubbed off on her skin, she realised. Pulling back the sleeve of her dobok, she showed her wrist band to the man at the desk and then wiped at her mouth with the sleeve. Her vision blurred and she staggered against the table.

'Are you OK?' he asked.

'Have to get to...' she began.

She couldn't finish the sentence. The world spun out of control and darkness took her.

Chapter 10 – You Should Rest

'Gee? Can you hear me? Are you OK?'

Gurveer's voice sounded insistent and worried. Gabriella recoiled from the stink of the smelling salts, turning her head away and coughing. A spike of pain seemed to drive deep into her skull with every cough.

'Woah! There you go,' a man's voice said. 'Don't try to get up. Just lay still for a minute. You had us worried there for a minute or two when you passed out.'

'Ow!' she groaned as she squinted up at the medic leaning over her. The man blurred in and out of focus. She closed her eyes again. 'Head hurts. Gurveer, go and get Kai. The man in black is here.'

'The man in black!' he gasped, his voice thick with fear. 'Where?'

'He grabbed me from behind when you went into the toilets,' she mumbled. 'I got away.'

'Man in black?' the medic asked, he leaned forward and sniffed the air just above Gabriella's face before looking at Gurveer for an explanation. 'She smells of anaesthetic. What's going on here?'

'Someone tried to kidnap her,' Gurveer replied urgently. 'I have to go and get my instructor. Please don't take her anywhere until I get back.'

'Don't worry,' the medic replied. 'She's not going anywhere. She'll be safe here with us.'

Gabriella closed her eyes and relaxed. Gurveer was going to get Kai. That was good. Once he knew the man in black was back, he would take care of things.

'Gee? What happened? I felt my ring get hot. Are you OK? We just bumped into Gurveer. He was frantic.'

It was Abi. Gabriella opened her eyes again to find her friend on her knees next to her. Abi looked terrified. Donovan was standing behind her, his eyes scanning the corridor for signs of danger.

'I'm OK,' she replied, looking round at the growing crowd around her. Her eyes held their focus this time and the pain inside her head was a little less intense when she spoke. 'It was the man in black.'

'Gurveer told us,' Donovan said, his voice sounding worried. 'And that you got away from him after he grabbed you. I look forward to hearing how you managed that!'

'Children, please!' the medic insisted. 'Give her some space. She needs air. Everyone move back.'

'It's OK,' Gabriella insisted. 'I'm feeling better now. My head is clearing. I want to get up.'

'Not yet, young lady,' the medic insisted, placing a gentle hand on her forehead. His palm felt cool against her skin. 'I'll be the judge of when you're ready to move. You there... yes, you,' he added, pointing at a nearby man wearing a black belt suit. 'Go to reception and have them call the police. Quickly! I don't think we'll need an ambulance, but whoever tried to drug this girl is dangerous. He can't have got far.'

The next few minutes were a bit crazy. The crowd grew as word spread of the attempted kidnapping. Kai arrived, followed swiftly by several of the senior Masters who had organised the tournament.

Kai knelt down next to her.

'Are you OK?' he asked.

Gabriella nodded.

'Was it definitely the same man we saw at the Oxtree Leisure Centre?'

'Yes.'

He took her hand in his and gave it a squeeze.

'I'm sorry,' he said quietly. 'I let you down. I shouldn't have suggested you leave the main arena without one of our black belts to keep an eye on you.'

'Do you know who did this, Kai?' a Master asked.

'I don't have a name, Sir, but I can give an accurate description of him,' he replied, his eyes never leaving Gabriella. 'I confronted him about three months ago after it was noted he appeared to be stalking some of my junior students. I didn't go to the police at the time, as I didn't have any real evidence to suggest he'd broken any laws. I've not seen him since. I thought we'd seen the last of him.'

Gabriella could see the lie in Kai's eyes as he said the last sentence. However, there was no hint of the falsehood in his voice and the Masters didn't question his statement.

'Bad business,' one of them muttered.

'I wouldn't have got away if it hadn't been for that lesson you gave us on breaking away from a grasp, Sir,' Gabriella offered. 'I did exactly what you taught us and it worked. I dropped straight out of his grasp and rolled away from his feet.'

'Good girl!' Kai replied, his eyes sparkling with delight. 'But he's fast. I'm surprised he didn't grab you again.'

'He didn't get a chance,' a man's voice interrupted.

Gabriella looked round. It was a member of the Leisure Centre Staff. She vaguely recognised his voice as that of the person who had shouted when she had started running.

'I saw the whole thing. This young lady is some piece of work! She swept that guy's legs out from under him so hard, he went down like a ton of bricks,' he continued. 'Smacked his head on the floor. I imagine he's still seeing stars now. It was the darnedest thing! I would never have believed that a young girl could take down a guy of his size. True, he was slim, but he was tall and certainly weighed a lot more than she does. I have a whole new respect for what you teach these kids, I can tell you!'

Kai nodded.

'Gabriella is one of my more promising students,' he said, giving her a warm smile. 'She listens well and works hard.'

'Well, it was impressive,' the man said. 'I was behind the front desk at the time. Before I had a chance to do anything, she was up and running. Then the guy was up as well. He seemed to consider chasing her for a second, but then legged it out through the main doors. I yelled for him to stop, but he didn't look back. If it's any consolation, young Gabriella, he was holding the back of his head as he ran. I think he's going to have some headache later!'

'Good!' she said. 'That stuff on the cloth has made my head hurt, too. I've got a really sharp pain, deep inside.'

'You should rest,' the medic said. 'Sit quietly for a while. The pain will go.'

'But I want to compete!' she exclaimed. 'I came for the sparring. I don't want to miss it.'

'You're in no fit state...' Kai began.

'I'll be fine,' she insisted. 'Give me a few minutes to clear my head and I'll be ready to fight. Please! Don't make me miss out because of that freak. I've got a bit of time left to recover before my competition, haven't I?'

Chapter 11 – The Final

Sparring in competition was not like sparring in class, Gabriella decided as she stepped out into the square to face her opponent for the final. Whether it was adrenaline, or the product of having been taught differently, she didn't know, but the girls here were kicking and punching far harder than she was used to.

One of the Masters had spoken with the senior referee on the square where her competition was being held. He arranged for her first fight to be the last of the first round bouts to give her as much recovery time as possible. This did give her a chance to watch most of the girls in action before she had to face up to her first opponent. Looking back, this had worked very much to her advantage. By the time she entered the square, she had a good feel for the standard and had mentally noted who the most dangerous fighters were among the rest of the field.

'Come on, Gee,' she murmured to herself. 'Silver is guaranteed, but you're here for gold.'

Staying light on her feet, she had easily outpointed her opponent in the opening round of the competition, picking her off time and again with simple front leg sidekicks straight up under her opponent's guard as she came forward. The frustration on the girl's face had become increasingly apparent in the dying seconds of the bout and she had charged in for a blitz combination that was too fast for Gabriella to counter or evade. The girl's back-fist strike had landed hard against her headguard – hard enough to set her head spinning again.

Blood had roared in her ears during the final few seconds of that first match, but she had kept her cool and simply evaded her opponent until the bell rang to indicate the end of the bout.

By chance, Abi had been her opponent in the second round, which had been a really fun match. They had kept the contact light, and fast. Abi was good, but Gabriella had the mental advantage going in to the bout, having been consistently better at sparring in class back in Oxtree. Despite winning comfortably against her friend, she couldn't help feeling it was a shame that only one of them could progress to the quarter finals with the way the draw had fallen.

The quarters and the semi-finals had been tougher, but she had managed to win both bouts without needing to change her tactic of scoring most of her points with front leg counter-attacks. The girl facing her now wouldn't let her do this. From what Gabriella had seen of her during her previous fights, she was an intelligent fighter who varied her techniques to keep her opponents guessing. She was flexible, fast and had a few centimetres height advantage. However, Gabriella had noticed a couple of the girl's favourite combinations that could be countered effectively if she was quick enough to spot them coming.

'Face me,' the referee ordered. 'Cheryots! Kyung ye! Face each other. Cheryots! Kyung ye! Fighting stance, chunbi. Free spar. Seejak!'

Gabriella decided to allow her opponent to bring the fight to her. It was what the girl would be expecting, as she had been careful throughout the previous rounds to give the impression of being purely a counter-puncher.

The girl came forward, bouncing lightly on the balls of her feet, her hands switching constantly between a high and low guard. Her blonde ponytail bobbed from side to side behind her.

'Come on, Gee!' Abi yelled from the side of the square.

'Go for it, Lana!' someone else called out. 'Chase her down!'

Lana, is it? Gabriella noted. *Which combination will you try first, Lana?*

She kept her eyes firmly fixed on the centre of Lana's body, refusing to allow her eyes to be diverted by the girl's constantly shifting hands. There was little warning of the first attack. Lana was good at disguising her movements. She pushed forwards, giving a dummy front leg side-kick and then immediately flicking her front leg up high to drop it down in an axe kick that Gabriella barely evaded. Before she could escape, Lana sprang forward and caught her with a back-fist strike to the side of her face.

'Hecho!' the referee ordered. 'One point, blue. Face up. Seejak!'

This time Gabriella gave Lana no time to wonder at the sudden change of tactics. Rather than back away, as she had done consistently throughout the tournament, she pushed forward from her mark, flicking out her trademark front leg side-kick. Lana was ready for it, but she wasn't expecting Gabriella to use her forward momentum to hop forward a second time. Before Lana had a chance to blink, Gabriella had whipped her leg straight up into a hook-kick that connected with the girl's helmet.

'Hecho!' came the order. 'Three points, red.'

'Yes, Gee!' Abi's delighted voice shrieked. 'You've got this. Keep it up.'

They returned to their marks. Gabriella looked her opponent squarely in the eyes for a moment, before returning her concentration to the middle of Lana's body. It was easy to see the anger in her expression.

She'll attack quickly this time, she thought.

'Seejak!'

Almost before the order to fight left the referee's mouth, Lana's leg was up and driving forward in a pushing side-kick, but this was exactly what Gabriella had expected. Rather than backing away, she spun, evading Lana's kick and firing a reverse side-kick straight up into her ribs. The girl's momentum carried her on to the kick and although Gabriella was not trying to kick hard, the impact of her foot against Lana's chest was solid and drew a gasp of pain from her opponent.

'Hecho!' the referee ordered. 'Two points, red.'

'Go, Gee! Go! Go, Gee! Go!'

Abi's chant made Gabriella smile. She shifted her gumshield with her tongue. It was not comfortable to wear, but she was getting used to it. Lana bent over for a moment to recover her breath.

'Are you all right?' the referee asked.

'Yes, I'm fine,' she confirmed, nodding. 'Just a bit winded, that's all.'

Gabriella felt bad for having hit her quite so hard, but at the same time she knew that Lana was likely to be a lot more wary now. The bout was only a minute and a half long and she was now holding a four point advantage.

If I can just keep her at bay now, the match is mine.

But the first few exchanges had happened so quickly that there was still more than half of the bout remaining. Keeping out of Lana's reach for that length of time was never going to be easy. Although she managed to drag out the next exchange, Gabriella eventually got caught by a turning kick to the body and her lead was halved.

'Don't let her control you, Gabriella. This fight is yours if you want it to be.'

It was Kai's voice. She hadn't realised he was watching. Just knowing he was there calmed her mind and her focus locked in tight on Lana's core.

'Seejak!'

They started again. This time Gabriella used her front leg like a probe, jabbing it forwards in a rapid sequence of side-kicks at Lana's mid-section and forcing her to back away. Breaking off her attack, Gabriella side-stepped away from the girl's anticipated counter, but she wasn't fast enough. Lana came in hard and fast, landing a solid punch to Gabriella's head-guard.

'Hecho! One point, blue.'

The margin was now just a single point. There was only a matter of seconds remaining. Defending such a narrow lead was no longer an option, she decided. It was all or nothing. They faced up on their marks again.

'Come on, Gee!' Abi was screaming.

Her eyes narrowed as she decided on her final tactic. There was a combination of kicks that she'd seen one of the black belts do in class a few weeks ago that had caught her imagination. She had practised them at home over and over. Although she felt she could do them quite well, she'd never actually tried using them during sparring as she found the combination sometimes made her feel dizzy.

Just do it! she told herself.

'Hecho!'

The order to fight triggered her into motion. Throwing a turning kick off her back leg that she knew was never going to reach, she landed the foot forwards and immediately spun through 360 degrees to throw another kick with the same leg, again landing forward and spinning. On the second 360 spin she jumped to give the turning kick more height, but again it missed. Landing forwards a third time she spun again, this time just through 180 degrees and flicking up a reverse turning kick that found its mark, catching Lana squarely round the side of the head.

'Hecho! Three points, red.'

At that moment the umpire sitting at the judge's table rang the bell to signal the end of the fight. She had done it! She had won gold in the regional championships! She bowed, first to Lana and then to the referee.

'Winner – red!'

The referee held her hand in the air to confirm her as the champion and Gabriella gave Abi and Kai a big grin as they cheered and clapped. She looked up into the stands where she knew her parents were sitting, only they weren't – they were standing and cheering as well.

'Well done. Good fight,' Lana said, pulling her into a congratulatory hug.

'Thanks,' she said, surprised by the gesture. 'It was close.'

'It was,' Lana agreed. 'You're good, but I'll be ready for you next time.'

Gabriella giggled. 'I'm sure you will,' she said, nodding. 'But I'll do my best not to make it easy for you.'

* * * * *

'Where is the girl?'

'I'm sorry, Master,' Driss replied, his head bowed and his heart pounding in his chest. 'She managed to escape. I'm going to need a bit more time. I'll have to wait for another opportunity.'

'Escape? You mean you had her and you let her go? What sort of incompetence is this? I pay you for results, Driss. This is more than disappointing. I expected better of you.'

'I apologise, Master,' Driss replied. 'I should have realised, given your interest in the girl, that she would not be an easy mark. I was not careful enough and she fooled me. I won't be caught off guard again, Master. I'll bring her to you. I promise.'

Master Chen crossed his arms over his chest, his eyebrows drawn into a deep frown. He turned away from Driss and regarded the cobra coiled in the nearest of the many tanks around his office.

'Very well,' he said coldly, 'But fail me again and you will take her place as the next test subject for my serum.'

Watch out for – Warrior Kids 4: Fearless